MW01147258

Will You ...?

Will You ...?

Sierra Welch

To order additional copies of this book, contact:
Xlibris Corporation
1-888-795-4274
www.Xlibris.com
Orders@Xlibris.com
98848

To Grandma Shirley, for helping me with my book.
To my mom, for being supportive.
To J.K. Rowling, for inspiring me to write.
To the Xlibris team, for making publishing fun.
To all my friends and family, for your sheer awesomeness. I love you all!

Chapter One

"Just *pick* one!"

Keiren Elton—a twenty four year old with a long, gangly build and brown, childishly floppy hair and equally childish rounded head—was beginning to get very agitated by his friend's hesitancy at picking out an engagement ring. Andon, the friend searching for a ring, was slightly shorter, with a lighter shade of hair as well as matching blue eyes. He didn't expect any less from Keiren's behavior. He never had been a particularly patient person, and the humid spring afternoon probably wasn't helping.

"None of them are right," said Andon.

"Right?" asked Keiren. "What do you mean, right? You're picking a ring, not the fiancée!"

"But none of them fit her," Andon explained.

"Resize them!"

"I didn't mean size," Andon retorted. "None of them *look* right."

"Again with the whole 'right' nonsense," said Keiren. "She's a girl. Get a sparkly one that won't turn her finger green and let's bail."

Andon continued looking. Keiren sighed.

"What about that one?" asked Keiren.

Andon glanced to the ring he was pointing to. "The band is too wide," he said.

"That one?"

"It looks like a deformed blob."

"That one?"

"I don't think she likes gold and silver mix."

"That one?"

"It has an amethyst. She doesn't like purple."

"She doesn't like . . . ?" Keiren took a slow, seething breath. "What about *that* one?"

"The diamond is too big."

"What?"

"The diamond is too big," Andon repeated. "It looks weird."

"*Please* tell me you're screwing with me," begged Keiren. "I think I just might shoot myself if you sincerely meant that."

"Would you like to go wait in the car?" demanded Andon.

"Fine," said Keiren. "Better atmosphere anyway."

Keiren stalked off. Andon returned his focus to the glass display case, trying to rule out each ring flaw by flaw. At this point, an employee noticed his struggles and stepped over.

"Hello," the blonde said perkily. "Can I help you?"

"I don't know," said Andon. "I'm trying to decide on a ring."

"Why don't I make a few suggestions?" the girl said. She pulled a key from her pocket and opened the display case, pulling out one of the many rings. "This is one of the most popular choices, at a very reasonable price. It—"

"Sorry," said Andon, "but I don't want a popular ring style. I want a unique one."

"Of course." The woman replaced it and pulled out a new one. "This is a one-of-a-kind ring that dates back all the way to the sixteenth century. The details are—"

"I'm sorry," said Andon, "but I don't want a gold band."

"That's perfectly fine." The woman's smile looked a little forced. She pulled out yet another one. "This is one of my personal favorites. It's very modern in style, and the princess cut diamond is sure to attract anyone's eye."

"My friend liked that one."

"He has very good taste," the woman said, beaming. "And you're in luck. For this week only, the price is . . ."

"I don't."

"Sorry?" the woman asked. "You don't?"

"Like it," Andon explained. "I don't like it. My friend did, but I don't."

All traces of a smile vanished from the woman's face. As she frantically searched for another ring, the bell above the door jingled. Not a moment later, someone unexpectedly grabbed his arm from behind and pulled him forcefully from the store.

"What are you *doing*?" Andon exclaimed.

"Good news," said Keiren. "As I was walking out of the store, I knocked into someone who was returning a ring."

"As fascinating as that is," said Andon, "I don't care about your reckless walking. It's almost as bad as your driving."

"That's not the end of the news," said Keiren. "When I ran into him, I knocked the ring out of his hand. We talked a little, and we came to an agreement on the price."

"Wait," said Andon. "You picked one without me?"

"Trust me, you'll love it," Keiren said confidently. "And more importantly, so will Tenn. Come on, let's go before we're late."

Andon opened his mouth to argue, then frowned and glanced at his watch. He was alarmed to see it was already six o'clock. He was supposed to be at his girlfriend's parents' house by seven and traffic could take forever!

"If you don't like it, you can propose another day," Keiren said persuasively. "But we have to hurry."

"Fine," said Andon. "But if I don't like it, I'll kill you."

"Fair enough."

They both got into Andon's blue Ford Taurus car. Andon started the engine and hurriedly pulled into the street.

"Do you want to see the ring?" asked Keiren.

"Yes," said Andon. "I want to see the stupid ring."

Keiren ignored the last bit of the remark and extended a black velvet box. While keeping his eyes on the road as best as he could, he flipped the lid to the box open. What he saw deeply surprised him. The ring's silver band had a very slim, fine shape. There was a cluster of diamonds carefully shaped almost leaf-like on either side of a dark, deep sapphire.

"Well?" asked Keiren. "Does she not like blue either?"

"You're right," Andon admitted. "It's perfect."

"Yes!" Keiren exclaimed triumphantly. "Ha! I have achieved the right to live!"

"She hasn't said yes yet," Andon reminded him.

"That wasn't part of the deal," said Keiren. "Even if it was, it won't be an issue. She'll say yes. Or realize only a complete utter geek would want to propose in front of her family and drop you like a sack of manure."

"Thanks . . ."

By the time they reached the house, Andon was feeling very jittery. He knocked on the door and rubbed his hands against his jeans, trying to wipe away sweat that had accumulated from his grip on the steering wheel.

"Well, hello!" exclaimed his girlfriend's mother, Mary, as she opened the door. "It's fantastic to see you two again! Come in, come in."

"It's great to see you as well," Andon said, giving a brief hug as he passed through the doorway along with Keiren. "Have you been doing all right?"

"Yes," Mrs. Crittenden said, "yes, of course. Tennley!"

Footsteps approached the living room, and a moment later, a girl in her early twenties walked through the doorway. She was wearing a simple white dress and had her strawberry blonde hair pulled back in a ponytail, exposing the freckles that ran along her cheeks and nose. When she caught sight of them, she grinned and hurried over to kiss Andon on the cheek.

"Hi!" she said. "I've missed you."

"I've missed you, too," said Andon, pulling her into a hug.

"I've missed you too, Tenn," said Keiren, extending his arms and grinning childishly. Tennley gave him a very brief one-armed hug and stepped back quickly before he could attempt something devious.

"Did you really have to bring your camera?" Tennley asked, looking at Keiren superciliously.

One of Keiren's quirks was his Polaroid camera. He carried it around his neck often, particularly to events. Andon had tried to talk him out of bringing it, but Keiren had insisted that he'd wanted to capture Andon's red face when he asked Tennley to marry him.

"I just thought I'd bring it," Keiren said casually. "Say cheese."

Tennley opened her mouth to object, but it was too late. The bulb on the camera flashed, capturing what was likely to be an awkward picture. Tennley gave him a penetrating death look and ignored him, turning to Andon.

"Tori's boyfriend just got here too," she said. "I'll introduce you to him real quick."

Andon nodded and let Tennley lead him to the dining room, where Tennley's sister and an unknown man were talking and laughing.

"Hey, Tori," said Tennley. "You remember Andon, right?"

Tori looked a lot like her sister. Both of them shared their mother's skin complexion and their father's light red hair. Tori's eyes were simply a lighter brown, her head was more rounded, and she was a good foot or so taller. She smiled when she looked up at Andon.

"Yes," she said, "of course. Nice to see you again. This is Brian. Brian, this is Tennley's boyfriend, Andon."

"Hello," greeted Andon.

Brian smiled and nodded, then returned his attention back to Tori in a captivated manner. Andon stood a little awkwardly, unsure of what to say. Luckily, Tennley felt the same tension and nudged him back to the living room. Tennley's mother had left, leaving Keiren alone. He was idly studying a glass case full of rifles.

"No-touch zone," Tennley warned.

"Yeah, yeah," said Keiren, waving his hand without looking around.

"I mean it," said Tennley. "If you break anything again, Mom will flip."

"That teacup was the stupid dog's fault," Keiren said bitterly.

"Just don't touch anything."

"Will do."

"So," said Andon, getting off the subject, "how are you and Sarah doing?"

Sarah was Keiren's recent girlfriend. They had been dating for almost three months, but Andon hadn't heard much about their relationship recently, opposed to the first month when Keiren never stopped talking about her.

"Eh," said Keiren. "We're all right. She keeps leaving messages on my voice mail because I haven't called lately."

"Maybe if you called her," said Tennley, "she'd stop leaving voice mails."

"Maybe," said Keiren. "Or it'll give her more of a reason to leave voice mails."

"How do you figure?" Tennley asked skeptically.

"We'll start a new conversation, and she'll make plans—like going out to dinner or something—and she'll have something to leave a message about," Keiren explained.

"Charming," Tennley said dryly.

"I try."

"Kids," Mrs. Crittenden called, "time for dinner!"

Tennley took Andon's hand, and they made their way to the dining room once again. Tennley's father, Spencer, had appeared and was talking animatedly to Brian. He gave Andon and Keiren a quick smile of acknowledgment and returned to his conversation. Whatever they were talking about, they seemed very enthused about it.

"Sit down," Mrs. Crittenden encouraged. "Help yourselves."

"Thank you," Andon said politely.

"Thanks," Keiren contributed brightly, beginning to pile his plate with mashed potatoes and pasta. Andon noticed he didn't so much as glance at the green beans that were laid out.

"It's nice that you five came up to visit," Mrs. Crittenden said cheerfully, taking a seat next to her husband.

"I like it better here than at my parents house," Keiren stated just as happily. "Crazy nut heads."

"I wonder how they always find something with you to argue about," Tennley said sarcastically.

"Tennley," Mrs. Crittenden warned.

"Beats me," said Keiren, which wasn't all entirely true.

"So you don't get along with your family?" Mrs. Crittenden inquired carefully.

"Nope," Keiren said simply. "We never have. I moved in with Andon and his family in high school. I haven't talked to my parents since. I think they might have moved."

"That's too bad," said Mrs. Crittenden, looking sincere. "Have you spoken with your family, Andon?"

"We do, on occasion," said Andon. "They live in Rhode Island now, though. They don't like the city. Anyway, I hear you have a new job, Tori?"

"Yes," said Tori. "It's fantastic."

"Where do you work?" asked Keiren.

"Cutz," Tori said. "It's a hair salon on the corner by the strip mall, near the elementary school Tenn works in."

"I think you should consider stopping by her shop, Keiren," Tennley advised.

"As if I need it," Keiren said, mockingly flipping his hair over his shoulder.

"Do you work?" Mrs. Crittenden asked.

"I'm a mechanic," said Keiren. "I tried working in an office for a while, but I never got that whole typing concept down."

"I find it astounding that you can weld something upside down with one hand, yet you can't manage to open a simple word document without spiking the computer system," Tennley said with a twinge of disgust in her voice.

"I'm simply talented," Keiren said, shoving a heaping spoonful of potatoes in his mouth. Tennley scowled at his table manners—or lack thereof.

"What about you?" Mrs. Crittenden asked Andon. "Where do you work? I don't believe we've ever spoken about it before."

"He's a stay-at-home best friend," Keiren said before Andon could answer. Andon kicked his foot.

"I don't work right now," said Andon. "I recently quit."

This wasn't the most honest of answers. Andon had been temporarily working in a restaurant until he could find a profession that would suit him. It went very well until his boss got tired of bad reviews coming from Andon's problem of mixing up orders. Luckily, his boss offered him a chance to quit before he got a record of being fired for improficiency.

Until he could get back on his feet again, his parents had offered to send money into a bank account monthly.

"That's too bad," Tennley said, though she knew the story fully well. "I'm sure you'll find something."

"Brian got promoted," said Tori, sounding proud.

"Is that so?" Mr. Crittenden asked Brian with interest.

"Yes, it is," Brian said. "I've become manager of my company."

"Really?" Mr. Crittenden asked, astounded. "That's a fantastic, chap!"

"What's your company?" asked Keiren.

"We make drills," explained Brian. "It's nothing too fancy, but it pays well."

"Drills, huh?" Keiren asked. "That sounds fun. Do I get a discount?"

"Perhaps," Brian said indifferently.

"Brian's got all kinds of plans," Tori continued in an upbeat manner. "He's going to move into a really nice part of the city and buy a house in the suburbs and . . ."

Andon was distracted by Tori's excited rambling when Keiren nudged his side and motioned for him to lean closer.

"You should ask now," he whispered, "while we're still on the subject of success and all. You need to one-up him."

Despite Andon's consistent planning, he felt his blood rush faster knowing that the time was so close. What if she said no? Would he leave? He couldn't just sit back down and continue eating. But what if it seemed rude if he left? What if he looked pathetic for staying? Why didn't he think of the worst-case scenario while he was planning? His hands fumbled with the velvet box in his pocket, which was becoming damp from his grip.

He waited a few minutes for a break in the conversation. Tori seemed so happy; he didn't want to interrupt her. When she paused to take a drink, he tightened his grasp on the ring box and started to stand. Now or never.

Before he could get to his feet, he noticed Brian stand and tap a knife against his glass to make an announcement. Andon sank back into his chair before anyone other than Keiren could see his movement.

"I appreciate that you brought all that up, Tori," said Brian. "It's funny, really. It feels so sudden, but now I have the perfect job, the perfect house, and the perfect girlfriend. But what I don't have is the perfect wife . . ." To Andon's shock and horror, Brian knelt on one knee. "Tori, will you marry me?"

"Yes!" Tori squealed, clapping her hands excitedly for just a moment before pulling Brian into a very passionate kiss.

While everyone shrieked and gathered around the newly engaged couple, Andon sat in a stunned state. He hadn't seen *that* coming . . . *Now what?*

Keiren realized the dilemma and quickly took charge of the situation by standing and saying, "I'm really happy for you two. I don't mean to be rude, but I need to talk to Andon in the other room."

No one paid them any mind as Keiren dragged him out of the dining room.

"So?" he asked.

"So, what?" asked Andon.

"Did you finally see how geeky it is to propose in front of the girl's family?"

"Not the time for jokes," Andon shot. "What do I do now?"

"Nothing," said Keiren. "Absolutely nothing. You'll have to propose on another day."

"What? I've been planning this for weeks!"

"But you can't follow *that!*" said Keiren. "You'd look bad! Plus, imagine the awkwardness."

"So, I just don't propose?" asked Andon.

"Not today."

Andon angrily ran a hand through his hair.

"Cool down," Keiren soothed. "You can propose later in the week, which will be perfect, because now her mind will be on marriage for a while. No worries. I'll help you come up with ideas."

"Ideas?" asked Andon.

"Well," said Keiren, "now you have a bar set. You have to be creative with your proposal."

"Andon?" called Tennley. "Keiren?"

"One sec," Keiren called back. He continued to Andon in a hushed voice, "Just smile and act normal. We'll work it out tomorrow. Trust me."

Andon agreed to follow Keiren's judgment, and they both returned back to the dining room. He supposed just one little snag in the proposal couldn't hurt.

Chapter Two

Keiren and Andon decided that proposing the next day would be too soon, so they ended up deciding on the day after. It seemed good enough. He'd been reluctant to let Keiren become involved with the ideas, but he'd given in when Keiren played the "best friend" card. As it turned out, Andon was surprised when Keiren actually came up with a good plan that was unlikely to involve injury. They were currently in Andon's apartment, packing a picnic basket.

"How are the cupcakes going?" asked Keiren.

"Pretty good," said Andon. They had bought a box of chocolate cupcake mix and pink frosting. Andon was just starting to carefully apply red sprinkles. "What about the sandwiches?"

"Perfect, obviously," Keiren said cockily. "I'm making them, after all. When have I ever made a sandwich you didn't like?"

"When have you ever made me a sandwich?" Andon countered.

"Lots of times," Keiren said indignantly.

"You have not."

"Have so."

"When?"

"Last month," said Keiren. "When we rented movies and ate junk food all day."

"You ordered Subway," Andon objected.

"See?" said Keiren. "I was so good you believed me."

"You seriously made those yourself?" Andon asked suspiciously.

"Yup," Keiren said proudly.

"Then why did you charge me twenty dollars?"

"You're getting sprinkles everywhere, Andon," Keiren said, getting off topic.

Andon glanced down at the counter, where he was, indeed, making a mess of the sprinkles. He returned his eyes to the task at hand. "You're an idiot, Keiren."

"Yeah," agreed Keiren, "but it's too late to go back now. So let's just forgive and forget."

For the next hour, they finished last minute plans, and Keiren gave him conversation tips. Don't remark on the weather, don't talk about his day, don't talk about anything but her, frequently compliment how she looks, and don't say anything that would make her want to push him off the Statue of Liberty. Andon didn't find it too productive of a conversation. The only thing he had to remember was where the cupcake with the ring was. They planned it strategically so he wouldn't be fumbling for the right one; it would be in the nearest left corner from the opening of the basket. Easy enough.

At twelve o'clock, Andon was on the fourth floor of Tennley's apartment complex. He knocked on her door, and she emerged a moment later.

"Hi," she said, greeting him with a kiss. "Wait right here. I just need to get my jacket."

She disappeared for a second. She left the door open, allowing the scent of Pine Sol and Febreze to drift down the hall. Andon always liked the smell of the apartment. It was always very clean and organized. Tennley appeared a moment later, covered in a lacey, see-through jacket that Andon frankly didn't see the point of, considering it was June. Tennley locked up her apartment, and then Andon took her hand and led her down to his car.

"So," said Tennley when they started off down the street, "where are we going?"

"It's a surprise," Andon reminded her.

"I don't get to know until the last second?"

"Correct."

Andon couldn't tell if Tennley was curious or not. She didn't seem annoyed, which Keiren warned was a possibility considering her precise manner, so that was a good start. They caught up on each other's lives since they had last seen each other (two days ago) as Andon weaved through they busy streets. It was only a twenty-minute drive to his destination.

"Central Park?" said Tennley when they came to a stop.

"Yep."

Andon reached into the backseat and pulled out the basket. Tennley grinned.

"A picnic?" she guessed.

"Yep," Andon said again, smiling with her. "Do you feel up to it?"

"Don't be silly," said Tennley. "Of course, I do!"

They climbed out of the car and entered through the gate, intertwining hands while walking along the stone pathway winding through the large park. Near a large fountain, there were a couple shade trees where they chose to lay the blanket. Tennley readjusted it afterwards, since he allegedly didn't position it right. It made him suspect obsessive-compulsive disorder, but he chose that this wasn't the ideal time to voice it.

"Too bad I didn't know it was a picnic," said Tennley. "I still have a lot of those tarts my parents sent home with me."

"There's plenty of stuff in here," said Andon. "We probably won't get through it all."

He lifted the lid, careful to make sure it was at an angle where Tennley couldn't see into the contents. He pulled out a few of the sandwiches Keiren had packed and slid the basket out of Tennley's reach. Tennley accepted the sandwich and moved closer, resting her head on Andon's shoulder while they leaned against the tree.

"It's nice out," Andon said, looking up at the nearly clear sky. He mentally cursed. One of the few rules, don't talk about weather!

"It is," Tennley agreed idly.

"How was your day?" he asked, quickly changing the subject.

"It was all right. No news since what I told you in the car."

'*Oh. Right . . .*'

"You look very lovely today," Andon said, hoping to make up for his stupidity by sounding charming.

"Thank you." Tennley smiled up at him. "You look nice, too."

"Not as nice as you," complimented Andon.

Tennley laughed and shifted a little closer. Andon wrapped an arm around her waist and leaned his head on top of hers. He noticed that her perfume smelled mint-like, which complemented the fresh smell of the leaves and grass, as well as the delicate green flowers on her dress. He'd never noticed the scent before. He'd never even heard of mint perfume, on that note.

"So . . . ," said Andon, "have you talked to your friend from Wisconsin lately?"

As it turned out, small talk was harder than he had anticipated. When he was picturing how the day would go, he imagined they would talk and laugh the whole time. Instead, Tennley seemed content to just silently enjoy the park. When it got too quiet, Andon would feel obliged to say something and blurt something stupid. He wished they could just skip to the dessert so he could propose and get over the awkward situation. Why did Tennley have to eat so slow, anyway? She nibbles more like a bird than anything else.

It was an entire half an hour later, and Tennley still hadn't finished the sandwich. She ate half of it, wrapped it back in the foil, and set it off the side. Andon quickly took his chance.

"Do you want a cupcake?" he asked.

"Maybe in a minute."

"Are you sure you don't want one now?"

"Yes," said Tennley. "I'm sure. I will take one later, though. I've been having the oddest craving for sweets lately."

They fell silent again. While Tennley watched the sky, Andon watched the basket. He wondered if he should try starting another conversation. Looking back on his lack of previous success, he figured it was probably for the best if he didn't. '*How long would it be until she wanted the cupcake? How long until it would be safe to ask again?*' He felt like he was failing at his part in this date. He waited a good ten minutes before the silence got the best of him.

"Do you want a cupcake?" he asked in false casualty.

"All right."

Andon's heartbeat increased a little as he reached over and pulled the basket nearer. '*Nearest left*', he reminded himself. He felt for the cupcake he had deliberately placed in the corner and pulled it out, already beginning to shift into a kneeling position.

But then he realized the ring wasn't on the cupcake.

He felt a brief panic, which he masked by setting the cupcake on his knee and turning once more to grab a different cupcake. He took the one in the right corner, figuring he had probably made a direction mistake. He only panicked more when *that* cupcake didn't have a ring either. He quickly replaced it and reached for the one in the opposite left corner.

"What are you doing?" asked Tennley.

"Uh . . ." Andon thought for an answer. "I made you a special cupcake."

He pulled out the cupcake that had to have the ring. Only, it didn't.

Knowing he would look suspicious if he placed that one back as well, he grudgingly gave it to Tennley. She cast confused glances between it and Andon's, probably trying to figure out what made it special. She thanked him nonetheless.

"These are good," she said. "Did you buy them?"

"I made them," Andon said absently, mind still on the missing cupcake.

"Aw, that's sweet," said Tennley. She leaned forward to give him a quick kiss. Her lips tasted like frosting, which distracted him for a moment.

"Uh, thanks." *Stupid!* He should just not say anything.

Tennley didn't seem to mind the dorky comment. She continued watching the area, seeming interested in a group of birds that had landed on the tree they were leaning on.

When she finished her cupcake, Andon took the opportunity to try the cupcake that lay in the final unchecked corner. His alarm changed to frustration when there was no ring to be found. He set it on his knee and grabbed a middle (and also ringless) cupcake, which he offered to Tennley. He had to eliminate the cupcakes so he could find the one with the ring without tipping the basket upside down and shaking it. It must have simply gotten jostled out of place. Thankfully, Tennley accepted the second cupcake.

Andon had eaten three cupcakes while Tennley was still on her second. That only left six more cupcakes that could have the ring. Four, he reminded himself. One in the corner had already been checked. He pulled out another cupcake and, this time, wasn't even surprised when it didn't have a ring. All he felt was a grudging dislike for that particular cupcake.

"No, thank you," Tennley said when he extended it to her.

"Why not?" asked Andon.

"I already had two," Tennley reminded him.

"They're small," Andon persuaded.

"It's really nice of you," said Tennley, "but I think I've had enough."

Stupid female daintiness.

"Just one more," Andon asked.

Tennley gave him a weary look, which he returned with playful puppy-dog eyes.

"Okay," Tennley said, rolling her own eyes.

Andon kissed her head and gave her the sweet. When she began to nibble on it, he returned to searching for the correct cupcake. Instead, he wound up eating his sixth. He began to feel a mix of desperation and anticipation. There were only three cupcakes left, two of which had the possibility of holding the ring.

"Will you take just one more?" asked Andon. The rich frosting was becoming too much for him to handle alone.

"No, thank you," said Tennley. "We agreed that was my last one."

"There's only two left," said Andon. "If we each take one, there won't be leftovers."

"You could wrap them up," said Tennley. "Or give them to Keiren, for that matter. It would make his day."

"Please?" asked Andon. "One more, I promise."

"No offence," said Tennley, "but you're acting rather strange."

"I'll stop if you take just one more," said Andon.

Tennley sighed. "Just one more."

This was it! He was going to find the one with the ring! He pulled out the first center cupcake his fingers brushed. It was plain. That meant he knew where the ring was. It was the last cupcake, with his luck, but he found it!

He fumbled around the basket. His hand swept the entire bottom, but only found one cupcake. It was the one in the corner, the one he had already checked. That couldn't be right. He searched blindly for another minute, but there was nothing else there. Just that one.

He removed it, thinking maybe it was a different cupcake that had gotten shuffled into that spot. It wasn't. It was the same one. The same exact—ringless—one. He gave it to Tennley and frowned at the basket, rechecking his mental math. He had made twelve cupcakes. This was his seventh and Tennley's fourth. That made eleven . . . *Where was the twelfth?*

After Andon had dropped Tennley off at her apartment, he rushed straight home, declining her offer to stay a while. As soon as his car was put in park, he bolted out so quick that he almost forgot to lock his car door. He dashed up the steps, skidded to a halt in front of his door, and fumbled for his keys. When the doorknob clicked, he thoughtlessly took a running step forward, only to bound backwards and topple to the ground. He stumbled to his feet and jiggled the doorknob. He'd locked it. Why had his door been unlocked?

His question was answered when he stepped inside. Keiren was still there, sitting on the couch with his feet propped up on the coffee table and his eyes glued to the television. When he heard the front door shut, he glanced to Andon quickly and stood.

"So?" he asked eagerly. "She said yes?"

"No," Andon said, hurrying to the kitchen.

"She said no?" Keiren asked. "Wow, I certainly didn't expect that. I'm sorry."

"She didn't say no," said Andon. "I couldn't find the . . ."

He found it. The cupcake with the ring was lying on the counter where he had left it, knowing it wouldn't be forgotten in plain sight.

Chapter Three

"I have an idea!"

Andon looked to Keiren, who had made the unexpected declaration.

"Your excitement makes me nervous," Andon admitted.

"No, no," said Keiren. "It's great. Would Tenn want to go to the hockey game with us today?"

"Probably not," said Andon. "She hates sports. Why?"

"I just remembered," said Keiren. "Once I was at a hockey game—it was just last month, actually—and during one of the breaks, this guy proposed to this girl over the big screen. Everyone thought it was romantic and the girl was completely won over."

"Was this story told to remind me about my failure yesterday?"

"No," Keiren said exasperatedly. "I'm telling you that you should bring Tenn with us and propose the same way!"

"I don't know," said Andon. "I would feel like I'd be stealing someone's idea."

"What? And a ring in the food is original? Come on! Loads of people have proposed over the screen before! No decent girl would refuse a proposal in front of hundreds of people."

"Doesn't that make it peer pressure or something?"

"Nah," said Keiren, waving an impatient hand. "Girls love attention. I'll call the stadium real quick."

He snagged Andon's phone off the receiver, hopped over the arm of the couch, and started dialing as he walked into the next room.

Meanwhile, Andon waited in the living room, playing over the possible outcomes in his head. He imagined Tennley's startled face when the screen's image focused on her with Andon kneeling by her side. There would probably be some kind of cheesy animation or decoration along the border. He wondered if she would cry, or if she would react like Tori did and look ecstatic. His thoughts were interrupted by Keiren reentering the room.

"I called the rink and Tenn," he said. "The stadium was more than happy to set up the arrangement, and I charmed Tenn into coming. They're going to hold her ticket at the front desk. I also called the car shop. I get to pick up my car today!"

Andon wondered how long he'd been spaced out to allow Keiren to make three calls.

"What car?" he asked.

"My new one!" said Keiren. "I just bought it. Will you drive me to the shop after the game? It's the last chauffer ride you'll ever give me."

"I don't see why not as long as you wait ten minutes after I leave the parking lot to drive it out."

"Great! Thanks! Well, come on. Let's go pick up Tenn."

Andon locked up the apartment, made sure he had their tickets and the ring, and drove off. Keiren hummed the entire time, not needing words to establish his happiness. When they got to Tennley's complex, she was already waiting outside. She climbed into the backseat of the car, and they started away again.

"Hey, Tenn," said Keiren, waving enthusiastically into the rearview mirror.

"Hi, Keiren," said Tennley. "Hey, Andon. Where's Sarah?"

"Why do you ask?" asked Andon.

"Isn't she coming, too?"

"No," said Keiren. "That's a ridiculous assumption."

"She said you haven't been talking to her."

"Since when do you two talk?"

"We have for a while," said Tennley. "Why don't you call her back?"

"Didn't we already have this conversation?"

"I'm still not quite grasping you."

"I don't think it will work out between the two of us," answered Keiren.

"So call her and tell her that," shot Tennley.

"Calm down," said Keiren. "I will. Tomorrow."

"Good," said Tennley. "Best phone call she'll get in her life."

"Sheesh, it's really good to see you again too," Keiren muttered.

The car elapsed into silence. Andon kept his mouth shut, not wanting to replay his stupid small talk from yesterday. Not another word was exchanged on the way to the hockey rink. The first words came from Keiren when he showed the man at the front desk their tickets and retrieved Tennley's as well. When the entered the bustling atmosphere inside, the tension lightened a little.

"Snacks!" Keiren established. "What do you two want?"

"Pepsi and a small bag of peanuts," said Tennley.

"The same," Andon said.

Keiren bounded away. Andon and Tennley waited where they were, and Andon took that moment of aloneness to wrap an arm around her waist.

"I missed you," he said.

"You saw me yesterday."

"That doesn't mean I can't miss you."

Tennley smiled. "I missed you too. So, who's playing today?"

"The New York Rangers and Maine Black Bears," said Andon. He was sure she was likely to forget the names anyway.

Keiren returned just then, juggling a large amount of snack products. "A little help, please," he said.

"Keiren," said Andon, "we just ordered peanuts and a soda. What's all this?"

"Mine."

"Why don't you weigh four hundred pounds yet?" Tennley asked as though he defied all natural logic.

"Because then no one would notice my stunning good looks," said Keiren, flashing his teeth in a wide grin. "Come on, take your things. I'm losing my grip on the sodas."

Andon and Tennley quickly took what they'd ordered, and Andon helped to take a few other items off Keiren's hands.

"Thanks, pal," said Keiren. "Would you lead the way? It's hard to see over the cotton candy bag."

Andon glanced once more at the numbers on his ticket and led them through a set of large doors into the dark stadium. He brought them both down the stairs until he reached their row, which was a little more than halfway down and—thankfully—at the end near the stairs. Andon couldn't imagine the trouble Keiren would have made trying to climb over people.

"Looks like you'll need a whole other row just for your food," Tennley commented as Keiren slowly sat down, careful not to let anything slip.

"Do you think they'd let me?"

Tennley rolled her eyes and rested her head on Andon's shoulder. He put an arm around the back of her chair, anxious for halftime. It was comforting to know he wouldn't mess anything up this time. Everything was set and planned.

They waited for fifteen minutes. During that time, Keiren had gone through a third of his armload of food. He had somehow irked Tennley, who had switched seats with Andon so he sat between the two and she sat deeper into the isle. Keiren leaned around Andon to stick his tongue out at her. Tennley scowled at him.

"Hey."

All three of them looked up when a large man with a tattooed scalp stopped to hover over them at the stairs.

"Pick your things up off the walkway, moron," Tennley told Keiren.

"No," grunted the man. "You're in my seat."

"We are?" asked Andon.

"She is." The man motioned—in a very rough and somewhat rude manner—to Tennley.

"No, she's not," said Keiren. "I paid for her ticket. There must be some sort of mix-up."

The man thrust a ticket in Keiren's face. Keiren tipped his head back and ripped the ticket from his hand.

"This is probably a mix up," he said confidently. "I understand. Sometimes, it can be hard to tell where to . . . Oh." He had pulled Tennley's ticket from his pocket and his eyes were glancing back and forth between the two. Andon didn't need to see the ticket to know there was something wrong with it.

"You reminded them to get adjacent seating," said Andon, "didn't you?"

"Ha-ha," said Keiren in a rather helpless way. "Uh, well, I thought they would figure it out for themselves, you see."

"Keiren," Andon groaned. Why did he have to have ticket strife *this* day?

"I'll handle it," Keiren whispered. He got to his feet. Despite Keiren's decent height, he looked rather inferior compared to the stranger. "Look, sir, I'm sure we can sort through this. Would you mind taking this ticket in exchange for yours? It's really important that—"

"I paid for this ticket," spat the man. "*Yours* is further back. One of you lot, go and take your seat."

"Can we step over there for a sec?" Keiren asked, putting a hand on the man's shoulders to guide him away. The man made a harsh, sudden movement which caused Keiren to react by jerking away and trip down a stair. Andon jumped forward to grab him, but Keiren managed to cling

Andon looked to where Tennley was gesturing. On the very ground floor, Keiren was standing next to an employee who was controlling a camera.

"Is he pointing at us?" she asked curiously.

It occurred to Andon what Keiren was doing. He quickly got back on his feet.

"I need to talk to him real quick," he said. "I'll be right back."

He hurried down the steps. Keiren had left the cameraman's side, and it was starting to get hard to keep track of his position. After knocking into several people and shoving his way through groups walking along the stairs, he finally caught up.

"Oh, hey!" said Keiren. "Why aren't you with Tenn?"

"Call me paranoid," said Andon, "but why were you talking to the camera crew?"

"They forgot to put you in their curriculum," said Keiren. "I figured it would look bad to Tenn if she saw you talking to them yourself, so I reminded them for you. You can thank me later if Tenn says yes."

"Keiren!" exclaimed Andon. "I canceled the on-screen proposal!"

"Why?" demanded Keiren.

"The topic came up with Tenn," said Andon. "She thinks it's tacky."

"Oh," said Keiren. "Sorry about that. I was so sure she'd think it was sweet. Well, this is an easy fix. I'll just go back to the person who's going to film you and . . ."

Keiren trailed off. He was staring with an unreadable expression at a point behind Andon's shoulder. Andon turned to see that he was looking at the camera platform, which was now empty of an employee.

"Um . . . That's not good," Keiren said.

With a feeling of dread, Andon rushed back up the stairs to the information center. He had a feeling this was going to be one of the longest days of his life.

Chapter Four

It had been two days since the hockey fiasco. Andon and Keiren had gotten everything worked out, with the request of the manager that neither of them ever contact an employee. It had been an acceptable negotiation.

The clock was nearing six, and Andon stood in front of a mirror, adjusting his suit. He had decided to take a more traditional route by putting the ring in a glass of wine, so he was taking Tennley out to her favorite restaurant, 1 Nocello. As he was finishing getting ready, he heard a roaring sound nearby. He had a strong hunch of what it was and pulled the living room curtains back to peer down at the street. Sure enough, his suspicions were confirmed. It was Keiren. After he had gotten his car—a convertible red Mustang—he had taken the habit of speeding by Andon's apartment complex, exaggerating the loudness of his car. Andon rolled his eyes at his show-off of a friend and closed the curtains as Keiren disappeared around the corner. He would be surprised if the car remained intact for a month.

Andon smoothed out his clothes and made his way to his car. He drove the familiar route to Tennley's apartment, and once she was in the car, he left toward the restaurant. He willed himself not to be nervous and to simply relax.

"You look very pretty," Andon complimented when he held the car door open for her to step out.

"Thank you," said Tennley, smoothing the front of her red dress self-consciously.

"Ladies first," Andon said, giving a dorky bow at the restaurant door as well. Tennley gave a playful half-curtsy and stepped in.

The restaurant looked very charming. The lights were dim, complimenting the colors of the room. Red roses were an excellent touch as a centerpiece of each table.

"You can sit down," Andon said. "I'll go talk about the reservation."

Tennley nodded and sank gracefully into a chair in the waiting area while Andon stepped up to a man behind the podium.

"Name?" the man asked mildly. He had dark hair that was slicked back with a large amount of gel.

"Andon Court."

"Reservation for two?"

"Yes," Andon confirmed. He glanced over his shoulder and lowered his voice. "I'm here with my girlfriend and plan to propose to her tonight. I was wondering if I could give the ring to your staff and have a waiter give it to her in a glass of red wine."

"That can be taken care of," the man said fathomlessly.

"Great." Andon fished through his pocket and handed him the small box. "Thanks."

"Of course," the man said. "You will be seated in a moment."

"Thank you," Andon said again. He returned to Tennley and waited with her another few minutes until they were escorted to a small table.

"It's very nice here," Tennley said, adjusting and fidgeting with her dress.

"I agree," said Andon, giving her a menu, half of which seemed to be written in a foreign language, and flipping through his own. "Perfect. So, have you been enjoying time off work?"

Tennley was a first-grade teacher. Andon had first thought her obsessive need for neatness would clash with her job, but she was very good with children. The school year had ended earlier in the month.

"Yes," said Tennley. "I miss the kids, though. You wouldn't believe the energy they had on the last day of school."

Tennley launched into an enthusiastic story of the behavior of the students that day, which had been devoted to arts and crafts as well as a lot of outdoor play. The story was interrupted by the waiter taking their order. Tennley paused while Andon gave him both of their orders and excitedly continued on when he left, not stopping when he delivered the food a minute later.

" . . . and then the boy actually *tried* to eat the macaroni he glued to his paper. While I was getting him sorted out, Lizzy tried pasting feathers to the wall! They can really be a handful."

"Sounds busy," Andon agreed. Just the thought of being around all the mayhem gave him a headache.

"So," Tennley said in a suddenly off-hand voice, "have you ever wanted kids?"

"Uh . . ." The question had taken Andon my surprise. "Maybe."

"I think you'd do well with kids," Tennley stated.

Andon wasn't quite sure how to reply to that. Out of the corner of his eye, he noticed a waiter heading toward their table with two glasses of wine.

"I'm sure you probably weren't planning on talking about the future today—Oh, sir, I didn't order this."

"He did," the waiter answered in a strong Italian accent. He gave a thumbs-up sign to Andon and walked away briskly. Tennley smiled uncertainly.

"Actually," Andon cut in before she could continue, "I think today is perfect for talking about the future."

Tennley looked relieved. "I'm really glad you said that."

"But before we talk," said Andon. He lifted his glass as a toast. They gently tapped the rims of their glasses together. Andon slowly drank from his and watched for her to do the same and look into the liquid. Instead, he received a flaw to the plan when she set if off to her side without touching it.

"Don't you want to try the wine?" asked Andon. "It's sweet. I know you don't like the strong kind."

"That's nice of you to remember," said Tennley. But still, she didn't so much as glance at the deep red liquid.

'*Just* look *at it!*' Andon thought desperately.

"Try it," he urged.

"I can't."

"Why not?"

"That's what I was going to talk to you about." Tennley paused and took a breath. "I'm pregnant."

What?

"What?" Andon asked dumbly.

"I'm pregnant," Tennley repeated, forcing a nervous smile.

" . . ."

"Well?"

"Well, what?"

"What do you think?" Tennley's eyes were piercing him so sharply that it was nearly painful, but all Andon could look at was Tennley's untouched glass.

Oh! Right! Opinion!

"That's . . . that's great! I'm . . . when did you find out?"

"Last week," said Tennley. "I've been trying to find the right time to tell you, but it feels like everything kept getting in the way."

"I get the feeling."

"Come again?"

"Nothing! I'm happy! Really, I am."

He decided now was the time to focus on Tennley's news. He stood and pulled her into a hug, kissing her cheek automatically. He could feel the cloth of his shoulder dampen and realized that Tennley was crying. Was that good or bad? The entire restaurant, who must have been listening over the quiet piano, burst into applause. The waiter hurried by while Tennley was still crying, snagged the glasses, and disappeared into the kitchen. Andon rested his head on top of Tennley's to hide his angst.

The claps settled down, and Tennley sheepishly broke the hug and returned to her chair, wiping the tears from her face and looking calm as though they'd never been there. Andon fumbled for a fancy napkin on the table and awkwardly tried to help her dry her cheeks.

"Check?"

Andon glanced up. The waiter had appeared again, holding a receipt.

"Yes," Andon said. He accepted it and gave his credit card to the employee.

"Oh," the waiter said, addressing Tennley before he left, "and congratulations about your baby. I'm sure you two will be very happy together."

"Thank you," said Tennley, giving him a watery smile. She looked back to Andon. "You really are happy?"

"Yes," said Andon, "of course. You shouldn't even have to ask that."

"But are you ready to be a parent?" Tennley asked uncertainly.

"What exactly do you mean by that?"

"Nothing," Tennley said quickly. "I just meant it's a lot of responsibility."

"Well, yeah," said Andon. "I know."

"I'm sure you do," said Tennley. "But it'll also mean that we both have to change some things."

"Like what?"

"Like my job," said Tennley. "We can't raise a baby on one teacher's salary."

"I can get a job," Andon said, feeling indignant.

Tennley smiled, pleased by the answer.

"And then there's the matter of where we live," Tennley continued. "It's not safe for children here."

That he wasn't going to go with.

"That's urban legend," Andon denied. "Lots of kids were raised here. I was raised here, you were raised here, and Keiren was raised here. We turned out just fine."

"I wasn't raised here," Tennley said, sounding somewhat tense. "I was raised in Oklahoma. And don't get me started on how the city's exhaust fumes polluted Keiren's head."

"Maybe we should talk about this a little down the road," Andon said.

"Okay," Tennley agreed. "But soon."

"We will," Andon assured her.

At that moment, the waiter returned.

"Sorry, sir," he said. "But there appears to be a problem with your credit."

"What?" Andon asked, hoping he'd misheard. "That's not possible."

"I'm sorry," the waiter repeated, "but we can't accept this card."

"You'll have to," Andon said stubbornly. "I don't have cash."

"We can't," the waiter said just as persistently.

"I have checks," Tennley broke in, pulling out her purse and beginning to rummage through it.

"No," Andon said with a feeling of alarm. "No, no, I can fix this."

Tennley ignored him, scribbled into her check book, and handed the sheet of paper to the waiter. The waiter gave them a smile, wished them a good evening, and walked away. Tennley stood, and Andon forced himself to his feet.

"You didn't have to do that," he said, agonized. "I could have worked it out."

"We're not in the Twenties," said Tennley. "It's fine."

"I'll pay you back," Andon insisted.

"Don't be ridiculous," said Tennley. "You do realize we'll have to work together now, right?"

Andon nodded, but secretly planned on repayment anyway. The greasy-haired man at the front stopped them on their way out.

"I congratulate you both and wish you well," he drawled, extending his hand to Tennley.

"Thank you," she replied, shaking the hand.

"And good luck to you," the man said, turning to shake Andon's hand as well. Andon noticed him slip the ring box into his pocket. He felt a feeling similar to bitterness at its presence.

"Thanks," he mumbled.

They left the restaurant with despair hovering over Andon's consciousness.

Chapter Five

It was hard to say whether or not Andon slept that night. The sun had come up in seemingly minutes after he left Tennley's apartment, yet it felt as though a million thoughts had gone through his head that would need days to be processed. Over and over, the same things passed through his mind. How was he going to handle a baby? Where was he going to get a job? Should he and Tennley be married before it was born to avoid any possible future conflicts? And then that's when he remembered—they couldn't get married until he stopped being a *failure* at proposing!

He couldn't find the energy to get up, so he tried to make up for his suspected lack of sleep by hiding from the sunlight under his pillow. It was shortly after this that he heard the familiar roar of Keiren's Mustang. He expected it to pass by, but instead heard a window-rattling shriek as it pulled to what must have been an abrupt halt. Andon sighed, gave up on the idea of sleep, and groggily got out of bed, running his hand tiredly through his dark hair. Almost automatically, he walked in a robotic manner to the living room, where he unlocked the door, and continued on to the kitchen to pour a mug of sorely needed coffee. He was pulling out his sugar and cream when he heard a jostle of metal, a click, and a thud from outside his door.

Frowning, Andon walked back to the door, which was now locked. It looked like someone was shaking it from the other side. Andon sighed. He unlocked it once again and moved to open it, only to have the door thrown in his face, catching him unaware and knocking him to the ground.

"I'm sorry," Keiren said, rushing to help him up before he had the chance to recollect himself. "That wasn't me, I swear! Something's wrong with your door."

"Where did you get a key?" Andon asked, blinking at Keiren's keychain and rubbing his aching nose.

"You gave it to me!" Keiren answered.

Andon frowned, trying to recall that information. "No, I didn't."

"But you would have if I'd asked, anyway," said Keiren. "Come on, sit down. Hey, you're making coffee. I'll get your cup. You go to the couch."

Deciding the frivolous key really wasn't worth the brain energy, Andon went with the plan and gladly flopped down. Keiren joined him a minute later, placing the mug on the table and splashing some of the coffee over the rim in the process. Andon picked up the mug and gratefully downed the coffee.

"Are you just waking up?" asked Keiren. "It's almost one."

"I didn't sleep much," said Andon.

"Long night?" Keiren asked with a smirk.

"Sort of."

"How'd the date go?"

"Tennley's pregnant."

"That's . . . whoa, what?" Keiren's face reflected that of an innocent bystander unexpectedly smashed in the face by a soccer ball.

"Tennley's pregnant," Andon repeated. The words felt strange on his tongue. Unreal.

"Are you serious?" Keiren asked suspiciously. "Is this some kind of April Fool's joke?"

"April was two months ago."

"Right . . . But you're really serious?"

"Is this really something I would joke about?" asked Andon.

"Well, that's great!" Keiren said, beaming. "You're going to be a dad! How cool is that?"

Andon smiled weakly.

"Pretty cool," he agreed tiredly.

"My best friend's getting married and having a kid," Keiren said, looking lost in his own happy world. "Too bad I couldn't have been there to watch. Was she surprised?"

"I think I was more surprised than she was."

"Huh?"

"I didn't get to ask her," Andon explained.

"Why not?" Keiren asked exasperatedly.

"I put the ring in the wine," Andon said dully. "She wouldn't drink it because she's pregnant."

"Irony," Keiren stated. "But not everything had to go according to plan. Why didn't you just take it out of the glass and ask her then?"

"I don't know," Andon admitted. "They took the glass away before I'd even thought of that."

"I have never met anyone who made proposing sound so difficult."

"You try it, then," Andon retaliated grudgingly.

Keiren snorted. "Right. As if I'd want to *marry* Sarah."

"You're still dating?" Andon questioned.

"Unfortunately."

"I thought you were going to break up with her?"

"I was," said Keiren. "I am. But yesterday she fell down the stairs and broke a few bones. Even I'm not so insensitive to break up with her in the hospital. She could be out by now, but she's making a rather big fuss out of it."

"I'm sorry," Andon said sympathetically.

"That doesn't matter," said Keiren. "We need to think of an easy, child-proof way for you to propose. Are you two planning anything?"

"No," said Andon. "She said she's going to be busy baby-shopping with her mom."

"How far along is she?" Keiren asked skeptically.

"I think she said a month."

"Does she even know the gender yet?"

"I don't think so," said Andon.

Keiren muttered something that sounded a lot like "high maintenance," but it was hard to decipher.

"What about a baby shower?" Keiren asked. "You could ask her then."

"In front of her family and friends?" asked Andon. "Nuh-uh. I'll pass."

"What about at her sister's wedding?" asked Keiren. "When is that, anywho?"

"It's next week," Andon reminded him. "And I don't like the sound of that either."

"Next week?" repeated Keiren. "Didn't they *just* get engaged?"

"Their whole relationship was rushed, from what I heard," Andon commented. "I think they met a month or two ago."

"Eesh," said Keiren with an unidentifiable expression. "That's not even enough time to learn each other's last names. Do you know when you'll talk to Tenn next?"

"Other than maybe on the phone, no," said Andon. "And asking over the phone isn't an option either. I was thinking of sending flowers and balloons, but that's not really talking, per se."

"That's perfect!"

"Come again?"

"The roses and balloons," Keiren said excitedly. "You can have the florist attach the ring to some flowers with a small card that'll say 'Marry Me' or something like that."

"Shouldn't I be there, though?" Andon asked. "You know, to give it to her?"

"No," Keiren said flatly. "No offense, but you mess things up. Ready to go?"

"Go *where?*"

"The florist! I haven't the slightest clue why Tenn calls *me* stupid."

"I'm not dressed," Andon reminded him.

"Well, get a move on," said Keiren. "Rise and shine. Be ready in five minutes or I'm leaving without you and you don't get an opinion in the flowers."

Being the pushover he was, Andon was sitting in the passenger seat of Keiren's car ten minutes later, gripping his door handle hard enough to turn his knuckles white. Keiren had the most reckless, spontaneous form of driving he had ever thought was possible as a technique. How he got his license was a mystery, but Andon suspected bribery or charm. They were six blocks from the florist when something suddenly hit him.

"Wait!" he said.

That had been the wrong thing to say. Before he could utter another syllable, the car slammed to a violent halt, throwing his head backward before slamming it back against the seat. His now-locked seatbelt was digging painfully into his chest and shoulder.

"What!" Keiren exclaimed.

"What was *that?*" Andon shouted.

"I thought I was about to hit some kid's puppy! Why did you shout?"

"I said *wait,* not *stop!*"

A car behind them honked loud and obnoxiously long.

"*Shut up!*" Keiren screamed hysterically. "I don't know what to do!"

"Go!" Andon said.

Keiren jerked the car forward without a question and drove them the rest of the shot distance, pulling to a stop without a scathe.

"You can't just slam your breaks on in the middle of the street," Andon lectured. "You're lucky there wasn't a car directly behind you."

"What the heck were you squawking over?" asked Keiren.

"It's nothing worth getting in a wreck over," said Andon. "I need to talk to my bank. Something was wrong with my card, and I only have a little bit of cash."

Keiren looked confused for a brief moment, then, without warning, he whacked Andon upside the head.

"Ow!"

"I have money, doorbell," Keiren snapped. "Did you seriously almost kill us because of that?"

"I don't want you to pay for it," Andon stated.

"Where's the ring?"

"Why?"

"Because I'm paying for it."

"No, you're not," said Andon. "It shouldn't take long to talk to my bank."

"Five seconds, or I'll knock the ring off you," Keiren warned.

"No."

"Five."

"No."

"Four."

"No, Keiren."

"Three."

"It'll only take maybe half an hour to go to my bank and sort everything out."

"I hate banks. That's what mattresses are for. Two."

"Keiren—"

"Two and a half."

"You're counting up, airhead."

"Huh?"

"Really, it won't be long," said Andon. "You wouldn't even have to get out of your car."

"How about you just pay me back after your Bore Convention?" Keiren compromised.

Andon sighed. He supposed there was nothing wrong with that.

"Okay," he agreed.

They finally exited the car and entered the small crammed shop that smelled highly of flowers and perfume. There were so many pots of flowers and small trees that they crowded around the walls and windows, making the room look dim.

"Hello," a bleach-blonde woman behind the counter said monotonously. "How may we help you?"

"Do you do deliveries?" Keiren asked, leaning his elbows against the counter.

"Yeah."

"We want to make a delivery to someone," said Keiren, "with lots and lots of flowers. Some balloons, too."

"Do you sell 'congratulations' balloons?" asked Andon.

"Yeah."

"Do you have something that shows variety and price?" Andon questioned.

Wordlessly, she slid a pamphlet across the table. Keiren snagged a pen as well and gave it to Andon for him to look through.

Andon carefully leafed through the pages, occasionally circling flowers Tennley had brought up before—lilies and roses, particularly—and circling a few balloon bouquets as well. After a little mental math, he totaled it to be a little less than eighty dollars. That should be easy enough to pay back later. At least, that's what he thought until Keiren took power of the pen and began circling numerous other things.

"What are you doing?" Andon demanded.

Keiren opened his mouth, but was cut off by the girl at the register.

"Excuse me," she said curtly. "I'm going to need you both to step away from the counter so other customers can get through."

Both Andon and Keiren glanced over their shoulders.

"We're the only ones here," Keiren said.

"Step back, sir."

Keiren and Andon exchanged looks, but took a few steps back nevertheless.

"Anyway," Keiren said, returning to their conversation, "I'm making it more impressive and wooing."

"I can't afford that," Andon objected as the pen continued scribbling.

"Everything beyond your purchase will be on me," said Keiren. "But this had better darn well work this time."

"How can *you* afford it?" asked Andon. "Are you running some kind of new illegal operation in your business? Be honest."

"It breaks my heart that you'd think that of me," Keiren said with a playful pout. "No. Not yet. I got promoted."

"Really?" asked Andon. "That's great! When?"

"A few weeks ago."

"Why didn't you tell me?"

"I didn't want word to spread," Keiren explained. "I was afraid Sarah would think I was actually worth something and going somewhere in life."

"But you are."

"Yeah, just don't tell her that."

Andon rolled his eyes, which Keiren returned with a trademark snigger. They returned to the counter to fill out an order. As it turned out, romantic things like flowers came easier to Keiren than it did to Andon. Keiren explained the situation to the employee and told them what time on what day the delivery would need to take place so Tennley would be there to open the door. Then he brought forward a vase from a display case that was filled with numerous red roses and a single white rose.

"I was thinking," he said to Andon, "that you should attach the ring to this white rose and slip a small card into the vase."

"That sounds great," he said, honestly impressed.

The cashier didn't give them any problems. She sat silently, watching them with bemused eyes and occasionally nodding when they'd give her details or instructions. Her lack of involvement made Andon a little worried about leaving the ring in her hands, but was slightly assured when Keiren asked for signed confirmation that they'd be handling it and they therefore claimed responsibility for its condition. Andon kept the box and left the ring around the white rose. He left the store, praying that nothing would go wrong.

Chapter Six

The torturous circumstance of this new arrangement was the wait. For two days, his ring would be in the hands of strangers. Two days! Did flowers even live in vases that long? He hadn't the slightest clue. For all he knew, the flowers were dried and brown. They'd be delivering his engagement ring on dead flowers. That's *horrible* symbolism for starting a marriage!

It was half after the time the flowers were supposed to be delivered when the phone rang. Andon sprang from his seat, senselessly smoothing back his hair. It had to be Tennley. Other than the occasional call from his parents, she and Keiren were the only people who ever called him, and Keiren wouldn't dare call now when he knew Andon would be waiting by the phone. The ID confirmed that it was Tennley. She had probably found the ring and was calling to talk about it. After taking a deep breath, he answered the phone.

"Hello?" he said.

"Hi!" Tennley's excited voice said. "I *love* the flowers! Thank you so much, Andon. You didn't have to do that."

"You're very welcome," Andon said, pleased. "How did you know they were from me?" This was his casual tactic of bringing up the card he had left with the ring. That had been the only indication he'd given that hinted they'd come from him.

"I had to sign a delivery confirmation form," Tennley answered. "Your name was on it."

Oh. Or not.

"Well," he said uncertainly, "I'm glad you like them."

"I really do." Was she going to bring up the ring? "I'll admit, I was getting a little worried."

"Worried?" asked Andon. *About what? The ring?*

"It's silly, really," said Tennley. "It's just that after I told you about the baby, you hadn't called, and I was concerned that you'd freaked out or something."

"Oh no," Andon said quickly. "It wasn't like that at all."

"I know," said Tennley. "Like I said, it was a silly thought. But in all seriousness, I did adore the flowers. And the balloons. They made my day."

They made her day because . . . ? Andon waited for her to bring up the ring. Nothing.

"That's great," said Andon. '*Could I have just said anything more stupid?*'

"I don't mean to rush off so soon, especially after such a sweet surprise," said Tennley, "but I promised Sarah I'd visit her. It's her first day home from the hospital. My taxi should be here any second. I just really wanted to call before I left to let you know I loved the gift."

Loved the gift and . . . ? No mention about the ring.

"All right," Andon said dejectedly. "Well, tell Sarah I say hi . . . Wait, when did you two start hanging out?"

"We don't, really," said Tennley. "But she's taking this whole thing pretty roughly. She was crying over the phone."

"So I've heard."

"Oh," said Tennley, "and please tell your snot-nosed friend to sort out his commitment problems before we *all* rip our hair out."

"Will do." That was a lie. He'd given up quite some years ago.

"Bye," said Tennley. "I'll call you later. I love you."

"I love you too, Hon."

He waited for a "And yes, I'd love to marry you!" Instead, the other line clicked off. Andon sighed and collapsed on the couch. He just hoped she would find the ring before she was dumping the plants into composition pots.

It was late when the phone rang again. Andon, who had been mindlessly pacing his house, quickly stood and picked up the call.

"Hey," he greeted.

"Hey," Tennley's bright voice greeted in return. "Sorry, it's so late, but I have great news!"

She'd found the ring?

"Really?" Andon asked fathomlessly. "What is it?"

"Well, maybe it's not *good* news, but Keiren proposed to Sarah! He must have sorted out his commitment problems!"

"I . . . *what?*"

"I was shocked too," said Tennley. "She didn't say when or how he proposed, but it must have been right after I left. I'd only been home for ten minutes when she called. I really can't believe she said yes. But maybe that means they've talked about their problems and won't be displaying such emotional roller coasters."

"Maybe," Andon said, still baffled. To his knowledge, Keiren had been ready to break up with her fairly soon.

"I hope that's how it is, anyway," said Tennley. "Make sure to talk to him about it."

"I most definitely will."

"It's funny," Tennley mused. "Almost all of my close friends and family are getting married now, but we managed to skip over that straight to a baby."

Ha-ha. Funny . . .

"Really funny," Andon lied, forcing a smile that wouldn't be seen anyway. He was suddenly aware of a grumbling engine, a screech, and a car door slamming. "Hey, Keiren just got here. I have to go. I love you."

They disconnected. Andon walked the phone back to the table in time to hear very rapid and loud knocking. He figured Keiren was likely excited or anxious about something. When he pulled the door open, Keiren's fist collided with his forehead, making him stumble back a few steps.

"Why can't you ever pass through the threshold in peace?" Andon hissed, rubbing his head.

"Sorry," Keiren said hurriedly. "We have problems. *You* have problems."

"What the hell are you going on about?"

"How hard is it to propose to your girlfriend?" Keiren demanded. "Really. Are you *destined* to not succeed?"

"I still don't have the slightest clue what you mean."

"I went to Sarah's house to break up with her," Keiren started to explain, "but somehow, she got your vase. She found the ring and the card and now she thinks we're getting married."

All the pieces slowly began to take shape in Andon's head.

"She can't have," said Andon. "I put my name on the card!"

Keiren reached into his pocket and shoved something into his hands. It was the small white envelope Andon had bought a few days ago. He pulled the card out to show him the name, but his finger froze above the letterings, which read:

Will you marry me?

There was no indication whatsoever of who had actually written the card.

"Oh . . ."

"What am I going to do?" Keiren asked desperately. "I can't marry her. I really just *can't*! I'll have to leave the country, move to Mexico, and change my name to Roberto. No, not Mexico. That's too close. I'll move to Switzerland. My name will be Earl, and I'll grow old making a living by growing lavender farms and making Swiss cheese."

"First off, Earl?" Andon questioned. "Does that even originate from Switzerland? And second, it would be easier just to break up with her. As a matter of fact, I need you to do that. You need to get my ring back."

"But you don't *know* her!" said Keiren. "She'll have a meltdown! She'll scream and cry and throw stuff!"

"I'd cry too if you moved to Switzerland and named yourself Earl," said Andon. "But seriously, *get-my-ring-back-or-I-will-hang-you*."

"What's it matter?" Keiren asked miserably. "You're destined to be alone, and I'd rather die than grow lavender farms and pledge peace anyway."

Andon gripped the back of his hair and started to pace, feeling his stress levels begin to rise. What if Sarah showed Tennley the ring before he could get it back?

"You can come too," Keiren offered.

"Keiren! Focus! My ring!"

"What about it?"

"I need it!"

"What am I supposed to do about it?"

"Break up with her!"

"Whoa! Inside voices!"

Andon took a few seething breaths and aimed for a relaxed tone.

"Sorry," he said, strained. "Here's a plan; I'll drive with you to Sarah's house and stay with you for moral support."

"I have a better idea," said Keiren.

"What, pray tell, would that be?"

"We break into her house and steal it."

"That's a horrible idea!" scoffed Andon.

"Yours is worse!" Keiren accused.

"How?" Andon demanded.

"She's on pain medication!" said Keiren. "She was already crazy to begin with; she could be a psychopath now for all we know! Everyone reacts to it differently! Who knows what it will do to her head."

"How are we going to sneak in, pull the ring off her finger, and sneak back out without being seen?" Andon demanded.

"How are you going to propose to Tenn with a cracked skull?" Keiren countered. "Because that's what we're both doing if we try going about this the 'ethically correct' way. I see where you're coming from. I really do. But I won't break up with her to her face. I refuse. And if I do it over the phone, then we'll never get the ring back. We'll manage fine. I know we will."

"We're not super mutant ninja turtles," shot Andon. "It won't work. It's on her *finger*!"

"That's my plan," Keiren said determinedly, "and I'm sticking with it. I'm going now. If you want to come and supervise, cool. If not, then I'll manage on my own."

"This is the stupidest idea I've heard in my life. We won't *can't* get away with it!"

"I can't believe I'm crawling through this stupid window," Andon grumbled.

"Shh!" Keiren whispered from inside Sarah's bathroom. "I think I hear talking . . . It's only her voice, so she must be on the phone . . . Or she's a nutter."

Andon tumbled onto the tiled floor and stood, rubbing his back. He suspected that it had hit the shower rod.

"Where does your master plan lead us from here?" he asked.

"We have to wait," said Keiren. "Do you have any dye?"

"As a matter of fact, yes. I carry it around in my—*no*, I don't have dye! What kind of stupid question is that?"

"Well," said Keiren, "I saw this funny movie where these kids poured dye into this guy's shampoo bottle. I just figured that if we had nothing to do, it would at least keep us entertained."

"You're unbelievable."

"Shh, I think she's getting off the phone," Keiren said suddenly. Andon leaned against the door with him to listen.

"Yeah," Sarah was saying, "I should be going. I have to take a shower and then start going through my bridal magazine . . . Thanks! Yeah, I'm very excited . . . All right, I'll talk to you some other time. Maybe I'll call to ask your opinion on something I find in the magazines. Bye!"

"Wait," Andon whispered, "did she just say she was going to take a shower."

"Yeah," said Keiren. "Why? Do you think she'll take the ring off first?"

"Maybe," said Andon, "but no, that's not why I ask. My point here is that we're *in* the bathroom!"

Keiren's eyes grew as large as a quarter. He looked frantically for some place to hide and began to drag Andon back toward the window. Andon forced him to a stop and pulled the door to a linen closet open. It was lined with shelves, but there was a large empty gap on the floor. He shoved Keiren into the closet, curled up on the ground, and shut the door just before he heard Sarah open the other door and enter the room.

They both sat with frozen breath until the faucet turned on and the sound of water could cover the sounds of their breathing. Even then, they breathed as shallowly as they could. It was only after a few minutes had gone by and Sarah had started singing that Andon dared to speak.

"I think it's possible that she might have taken the ring off," he whispered. "It might not fit her and could fall off in the water. Check and see if it's by the sink."

"Me?" Keiren whispered. "Why me?"

"She's your girlfriend," said Andon.

"Pitiful."

"You're nearest the doorknob."

"No, I'm not. You pulled it shut."

Andon grit his teeth. Knowing there wasn't time to waste, he took a breath and slowly cracked the door, centimeter by centimeter, until he could see the sink through the sliver of a crack. His heart gave a small jolt when he saw, as luck had it, the ring lying on the counter.

"It's there!" Andon whispered.

"Good!" Keiren breathed. "Grab it!"

"I can't," Andon replied worriedly. "The shower has a sliding glass door. What if she sees me?"

"What if you don't do it and you never get the ring back?" Keiren tormented.

"Can't you do it?" Andon begged. "At least you could make up some story if it's you she catches."

"You can make up a story," Keiren insisted.

"Not a good one."

"You have to get out of the closet eventually."

"Not a time for jokes," Andon snapped.

Andon could see a shadow of a smirk on Keiren's face. Keiren gave him a nudge, and Andon mustered every nerve in his body and continued to slowly open the door. To his advantage, the room was very steamy and the glass doors were fogged. He crawled across the small space, snatched the ring, and quickly darted back inside the closet, pulling it shut. He was greeted with a triumphant high-five.

The wait afterwards was more relaxed. They leaned against the back of the wall as comfortably as they could and listened as Sarah shut the water off and bustled about the bathroom. It took a couple minutes until sounds of movement gave a long pause that was followed immediately by the noise of objects shifting around and drawers rapidly opening and closing. There was a gasp and then running footsteps out of the room.

"I think she noticed," Keiren breathed.

"You think?" Andon retorted.

There was a sudden loud buzz that made them both jump. Andon bit his lip after hitting his head on the shelf. He glared at Keiren, who seemed to be the source of the noise. Keiren fumbled through his pockets and extracted a large black cell phone.

"It's her!" he whispered. "What do I do?"

"Er, I don't know!" Andon said. "Just make that noise stop!"

Keiren fumbled with it, then froze and stared at it in horror.

"I accidentally picked up!" he whispered.

"Well, talk!" said Andon.

"Uh, hi," Keiren whispered into the phone. "What's up? . . . I'm sure you didn't lose it. It's probably lying around somewhere . . . Are you sure? . . . I'm not whispering. I'm just sick . . . Well, maybe you should check the bathroom again."

Andon, who had been listening to both Keiren and Sarah's voices, smacked Keiren's arm and made "stop talking" gestures.

"Oh! Uh . . . I have to go. Call me when . . . if . . . when! . . . you find the ring. Bye."

Keiren hung up not a moment too soon. They heard Sarah enter the bathroom again and resume rummaging. Andon gave a soundless sigh and tipped his head against the wall, eyes shut.

Three hours. They'd been in the stupid closet for three hours before Sarah had left the bathroom for the final time and disappeared into her room, likely drained from all the limped running she'd been doing. This made it possible for Andon and Keiren to sneak out the window. Andon's conscious had nagged him the entire time until he resolved to order her chocolate or something later on.

Andon was exhausted by the time he got home. He would have fallen asleep completely clothed, but his back and neck was killing him from being hunched over for so long. He trudged through a quick shower, willing the steam and hot water to help. It did, considerably, and he went to his room and flopped on his bed.

No sooner did his head hit his pillow did the phone ring. He groaned, very well considering ignoring it. But with a sigh, he reached and picked it up, not bothering to open his eyes.

"Hello?" he yawned.

"Hey, Andon," said Keiren.

"Didn't we just leave each other?"

"Yeah," said Keiren. "Just calling to say I finally did it."

"Hired a brain surgeon?"

"Nope," said Keiren. "Better. I broke up with Sarah."

Andon grit his teeth. "If you were going to break up with her today anyway, why couldn't you have done it and at least *tried* to get the ring back before we had to go through all that?"

"I didn't think it was too bad," said Keiren. "It was kind of fun, even. It was like playing ninjas. Hey, did you ever wonder if it wasn't fate, but Tennley that's getting in the way of your proposal? I was thinking about how the flowers got to Sarah's house. Maybe she found the ring, but was too polite to say no, so she took the va—"

Andon shut the phone off, rolled over, and fell asleep.

Chapter Seven

A few days went by. Tennley's sister was getting married in three days and Andon was running low on time, as it was his plan to propose before the wedding. Keiren had made a good point when saying anticipation of the marriage would have Tennley constantly thinking about love. The problem was that Andon was also running low on ideas.

His inspiration was finally sparked at the most random of moments. One day, while he was glumly sitting on his couch and channel surfing, something caught his eye. It was a commercial for Zales, a jewelry business. Normally, he would have just continued searching for a show that he recognized, but something kept his interest. In the commercial, a girl was sleeping with a string tied to her finger. Just across the street, a man stood on an apartment roof holding the other end of the string. He tugged the string to wake her up. Once she was standing at the window, he looped the ring around the thread and it slid down to the girl below.

It was as though a light bulb went off in Andon's head. That was perfect! He could do that! There was no risk of it being swallowed, looking uncreative, being lost in flowers, or ending with him being humiliated in front of other people! He glanced at his watch. It was just after six in the afternoon. Should he do it today? If he did, he could probably manage to do it before sunset. But would it seem desperate to spontaneously jump at an idea?

He was beyond desperate. After quickly grabbing the ring, he dashed out the door and caught a taxi. It was just after rush hour, and driving himself would be on the verge of impossible.

"Can you take me to the nearest craft store and stop for a minute while I run inside?" he asked the taxi driver.

"You're paying," said the driver. "Why not?"

Andon still had a small amount of cash left in his wallet. It was only twenty dollars, but it should be enough to buy string and still get to Tennley's complex. It would come close, though. He rushed through the craft store as quickly as possible, keeping in mind that the waiting taxi was still charging him for parking. Clear, transparent string was five dollars. He gave what was left to the taxi driver as he stepped into the backseat and gave him directions to Tennley's house.

"Will that amount get me there?" asked Andon.

"We'll find out," the driver said indirectly.

The taxi slowly veered back into traffic and inched down the street. Andon checked his watch after ten minutes, contemplating whether it would be quicker to walk. Before he could make the choice of canceling the ride, the driver pulled off to the side of the road.

"Your money capacity is up," he stated plainly.

Without a word of thanks, Andon hurriedly stepped out of the taxi and walked at what was probably a quicker pace anyway. He dodged around crowds, trying to race the descending sun. There was little chance that he would be able to pull it off in the dark.

It was after seven by the time he fought through the people and got to Tennley's complex. Andon walked in circles around it, mentally picturing where her window would be. He identified it as being the third window to the left on the sixth story. The fire escape led him up to Tennley's window, which was cracked. He knelt to the side of it. There was a glare reflecting off the glass, preventing him from being able to directly see if she was in the room and able to see him. But from what little he could see, the room was empty. Before that could change, he tied a loop at the end of the string—repeatedly knotting it, just in case—and looped it around a latch on the inside of the window. He dropped the other end of the string off the edge of the fire escape and started crawling back down.

The string unraveled itself as it fell to the ground. The alley between the two complexes was caught in the shadows, making it difficult to find. He squinted and searched for the clear string and finally spotted a clump of it on the ground. Andon lunged for it, as though it would catch in the wind and blow away. Now that he had gotten it *down*, all he had to do was get it *up*. He did what the guy in the commercial did; he wound it up as tight as he could and threw it with all his strength toward the roof.

It traveled several feet up and plummeted straight back to the concrete. Stupid television.

He resorted to his own plan—to tie the string to the bars of each platform as he crawled up the fire escape. He had to pass through a cut hole at each level, but he couldn't carry it up with him and still create a straight line to Tennley's apartment. It wasn't too difficult, but it was time consuming. He had to stop to untie the string, attach it to the next level, and then do the same all over again.

Twenty minutes later, the sun burned brightly and the clouds were tinting with bright colors. Andon pulled himself over the edge of the roof and, panting, looked down upon the sunset. His hands gripped the string so tight that it could have easily sliced his skin if someone tugged it. If he were to let it slip now, the string would disappear into the dark alley and make it nearly impossible to try again. Using one hand to maintain his death grip, he used his spare hand to retrieve the ring and loop it around the string, holding it in place with his thumb. Next, he quickly grabbed his cell phone and dialed Tennley's home number. At this time of the day, she should be home. The phone rang and rang. Just when he thought he would have to hang up and try again, the obnoxious ringing came to a stop.

"Hello?"

"Hey!" Andon said in relief. "Where are you?"

"I'm at home," said Tennley. "Why?"

"Go to your window," said Andon. "The one in your living room."

"Why?"

"Just go."

There was a pause. "That's a nice sunset."

"Look on the roof across the street." It was beginning to feel like a game.

Another second of silence, and then, "Is that *you?*"

"Yep," Andon said, beaming. "One second."

Andon propped the phone between his shoulder and ear. His hands were shaking, but he managed to pull the string to tighten his diagonal path. He then released the ring, watching it successfully slide out of sight. It had worked!

"What are you doing up there?" asked Tennley. "I can barely see you with the sun behind your back."

"Wait one second," said Andon. He could practically hear the reluctance in Tennley's silence. When she made no comment on the ring, Andon broke in. "Do you see anything at your window?"

"No," said Tennley. "Should I? Andon, what are you doing? Why have you been acting so odd lately?"

"You don't see anything at all?" Andon asked. "What about string? Is there anything tied to the inside of your window?"

"No. Andon—"

"Sorry," said Andon, "I have to go. Love you, bye."

"Wait, Andon . . . !"

But Andon had already hung up and was putting the phone back in his pocket. Once again, he had to go through the trouble of winding the string down correctly. He couldn't drop it over the edge without risking the ring falling off. If it was still attached, that is . . .

To his surprise—or, more specifically, confusion—the string was still attached to the window, which was now closed, by the time he reached the opposite building. The sinking sun no longer inflicted a glow on the window, allowing him to better see into the room. What he saw made his heart sink.

It wasn't Tennley's apartment. The ring was inside the unfamiliar apartment, lying on the window sill.

He scanned the room frantically. No one was there, so he took his chance, planning to quickly open the window, grab the ring, and run. He gave the window a tug. Locked!

Movement in the corner of the room shot a jolt of electricity through Andon's heart. He ducked, making a "*clang*" as the palms of his hands hit the platform. He held his breath in anticipation and gained enough courage to—ever so slightly—raise his head to peek into the room again. A few people were walking around, looking dressed up and preparing to leave. Sure enough, after a few minutes of careful watching, they would be out of the front door.

Now what should Andon do? Run and try to catch them at the front doors? Wait outside their apartment for them to come back? What if they just laughed at him? No, no, those weren't good ideas at all. Maybe he could force the window open. It was bold and possibly a little outrageous, but why not? It was worth a try, at least. It's not like he was breaking and entering. It was *his* ring, after all.

He tried what he'd seen Keiren do countless times; he retrieved his credit card from his wallet and slid it under the bottom window panel. To his frustration, it slid cleanly along the narrow gap, not catching a snag of any sort. It was times like this when Andon valued Keiren's mischievous intellect.

Andon was stumped. If that didn't work, what would? For what felt like the longest time, he sat and stared, considering his options. Using the card to unlock their front door would probably get him inside, but he didn't trust himself to pick the right door, especially considering the fact that he'd previously thought this was Tennley's apartment. So, there was no real option other than to go to the main entrance, wait, and hopefully recognize the tenants.

He stood grudgingly and began to walk away. Or tried to, anyway. He hadn't taken a single step when his left foot was jerked back. It was now dark and difficult to see, but he realized that his foot was caught on the string. He tugged his foot, trying to free it or at least snap the string. The harder he pulled, the more entangled he seemed to become. He lashed out at the string, kicking it violently. To his satisfaction, he thrashed out of it, snapping the string. He suddenly felt himself lose balance and—

SMASH!

In a fraction of a second after he stumbled, his elbow had collided with the window. He jammed his eyes shut and breathed rapidly, trying to imagine that he hadn't just heard a crack, and when he opened his eyes again, the window would be in one, perfect piece. Once he had convinced himself that the window was whole, he slowly turned to look at it.

Nope. It was most definitely broken.

Now what was he supposed to do? Should he leave a note with his name and phone number on it? No, that's stupid. They'd call the police. What he would do is come back in a few days and slide the money under their door. Yes! That's what he'd do. Before anyone could se him, he started off, keeping his head down.

Wait! he thought. *The ring!*

He sprinted back and checked the string tied to the window. It was still there, but the ring was not. It was lying on the floor a few feet below the window. Without a thought, he bent over the windowsill and stretched his arm, straining to grab the ring or even brush it with his fingertips. But it was to no avail; his arms simply weren't long enough. Andon heaved himself further onto the window until he was practically entirely inside anyway. He was close enough now. He extended his hand to grab it and get out of there, but he soon heard,

"*Brad!*"

An ear-splitting shriek gave Andon enough of a shock for his hand to slip, sending him crashing face-first into their living room. He heard running footsteps coming nearer and quickly scrambled to his feet, grabbing his ring in the process.

"No, it's all right!" he screamed after the woman who had shrieked as she disappeared around a corner. He ran after her in a blind panic, sure she was bound to call 911. "I'm not a burglar! This is a misunderstanding! I . . . !"

The last thing he saw after he turned the corner was a glimpse of a very large man. Before he could explain the situation, a fist connected with his eye, and all went black.

Andon's head throbbed sickeningly. With a lot of pained effort, he was able to force his eyes open. He was lying on a bed in a small, gray-stoned room with bars along a non-existing wall. It took a few moments with the headache, but it dawned on him where he was. He was in a jail cell.

He sat up abruptly, immediately regretting it when the blood rushed to his brain. Andon blinked rapidly, trying to clear the fog glazing his eyes. How did he get here without waking up? Better yet, how long had he been out?

"Excuse me," Andon called to a police officer who was a short distance away. His voice sounded hoarse, so he quickly cleared it. "Excuse me, sir. What am I doing here?"

The police officer, who trudged over to his cell, looked like someone who held much disdain for his job and, judging by the permanent-looking scowl engraved on his face, maybe life in general. He shifted a toothpick around his back teeth while he frowned at the papers attached to his clipboard.

"Breakin' an' enterin'," he grumbled.

A 75 watt light bulb clicked in Andon's head.

"Oh!" he exclaimed. "No! That's not what happened. You see, I accidentally broke the window. I didn't break in. And I was only in the apartment in the first place because I dropped my ring when the glass shattered and—"

"Yer trial will begin nex' week," the police officer said dryly.

"Shouldn't I be allowed a trial before I'm put in jail?" asked Andon.

He didn't know whether to officer's reply was relevant or not, but he said, "You can make a phone call."

The officer rattled with the bars and pulled them open. Andon stumbled when he got to his feat, managing to get a grip on the wall until his head cleared. He forced himself to take one step after another, following the police officer to a phone hooked on the wall. He muttered a "thanks" and stared at the dial. Calling Tennley was out of the question, so he dialed the number of the one person he knew he could rely on.

The phone rang. And rang. And rang. And rang . . .

"Hello," he heard Keiren's voice say.

"Hey," said Andon. "Look, I can't talk long, but—"

"I'm not at the phone right now, but leave a message, and I might get back to you."

Andon sighed in frustration. Stupid personalized answering machines.

"Keiren," he stated again. "Hey, I need you to do me a favor. I'm in jail right now—I don't really know which one—and—"

"Whoa!" a voice exclaimed from the speaker, startling him. "You're in jail? What the heck did you do?"

"I thought this was an answering machine?" Andon demanded.

"I was kidding."

"This is serious!"

"I didn't know that!"

Andon sighed again.

"Where are you?" Keiren asked urgently. "Are there any signs around or someone you can ask?"

"I dunno." Andon scanned the walls. Across the room from the main entrance was a large sign. "North Street Police Department," he said.

"The one near Tenn's place?"

"Yeah."

"Did you propose and she called the police?"

Andon could hear the smirk in his voice. "Not funny," he said flatly.

"Beg to differ," said Keiren. "Don't worry. I'm on my way."

"Thanks," said Andon. "Really, thank you."

"Don't mention it," said Keiren. "Expect to return the favor one day. See you soon. Then you're telling me everything."

"See you."

Andon returned the phone to the hook and was led away by the police officer to be placed back in his cell and fill out some papers until Keiren could get there.

Chapter Eight

Andon felt like he sat there for *hours*. He even had time to take a brief nap and rest his head. *Where* was Keiren?

After a lot of anticipation and waiting, Andon finally picked up on the sound of Keiren's very distinguishable laughter. He sat up and listened to him getting nearer. A few minutes later, he stood outside his cell with an attractive blonde police officer. Before Andon had time to think, a flash of Keiren's Polaroid camera set off. Andon glared and rubbed his eyes.

"Never thought I'd see the day!" Keiren declared. "*I* haven't even been locked up yet!"

"I haven't been locked up," Andon snapped. "I've been temporarily detained."

"Aw," said Keiren, "wipe the long face. Smile!"

Another flash. Andon's scowl deepened.

"Ready to go, pal?" Keiren asked cheerfully.

"Ready to leave, yeah," Andon mumbled.

The female officer unlocked his cell and escorted them out of the building. Andon tried to ignore the continuous clicks and light from Keiren's camera. When they stepped outside, Andon inhaled a lungful of night air as though it had been years since he'd last experienced fresh oxygen.

"All right," said Keiren, "get in the car and start talking."

Andon did as told and climbed into the passenger seat of Keiren's Mustang. As thankful for Keiren as he was, he wasn't looking forward to his driving tactics straight after getting out of jail.

"Shoot," said Keiren. "Well, not really. We're still on police property."

"Ha," Andon said with a roll of his eyes. "I tried to propose to Tennley again."

"Did she really call 911?" Keiren asked with a look of shock.

"No," said Andon. "I accidentally broke into someone's house."

"You've lost me," Keiren stated.

Andon launched into the story of how he'd seen the commercial on TV, how he'd thought it was charming, and how he'd tried to pull it off. He talked about how he'd attached it to the wrong apartment, gotten stuck on the string, and how he'd fallen into the living room and been knocked unconscious. Keiren listened and watched patiently with a look of understanding and sympathy. Andon thought it was comforting, considering his friend rarely had any form of a serious expression on his face. When Andon was finished talking, he started breathing heavier, trying to regain oxygen. There was a minute of awkward silence, which was broken when Keiren started roaring with laughter.

"What's so funny?" Andon demanded.

"Most people go to jail for theft or assault." Keiren laughed. "*You* go to jail for falling through a window."

Andon punched Keiren's shoulder, which only made him laugh harder.

"It's not funny," he said irritably.

Keiren continued laughing, clutching at his sides and doubling forward so his floppy near-shoulder-length hair covered his face. Andon smiled at his ridiculousness and found that he couldn't help but laugh along with him.

"Good night," Keiren called to Andon as he stepped out of the car. "Have fun, my dear criminal of a friend. But not too much fun. You won't get away with it."

He laughed and sped off. Andon smiled and shook his head while he walked through the front doors. He tiredly entered his apartment and was making his way to his room when a movement caught his eye, making him stop in his tracks.

"Hello, Andon."

It was Tennley. She had just stood from the couch, jaw set determinedly.

Uh oh . . .

"Er, hi, Tenn," said Andon. "Uh, what are you doing here?"

"I heard you went to jail."

There was something strained and hard in Tennley's voice. Andon could tell by the way she stood that she was very on edge.

"Oh," Andon said stupidly. *Think!* "How?"

"I saw you being taken away," Tennley said. "Why were you in jail, Andon?"

"Uh, that's a long story," said Andon.

"So you're just not going to tell me?" Tennley demanded, stepping closer.

"It was a . . . a mistake," Andon insisted. "A misunderstanding. I'm out for now."

"'For now?' You're going back?"

"Yes," said Andon. "I mean no. Kind of. I just have to go to some trial and—"

"Trial? You're going on *trial?* For *what?*"

"Breaking and entering," said Andon. "But—"

Without warning, Tennley grabbed her purse and threw it at him. Andon ducked, and it collided loudly with the wall. Its contents spilled everywhere. Andon stood up straight and swallowed. Never once had he seen Tennley lose her temper.

"What's gotten into you?" she exclaimed. "What, Andon? I want to know why you've been acting so out of character. You're always running off or acting like you're hiding something. You've been tense and fidgety. Your card bounced. You sent congratulation flowers but didn't make a single gesture of planning for the baby's—"

"I *just* found out!" said Andon, clenching his fists. "We don't even know the gender yet! How can we plan until we know what colors of clothes to even buy?"

"Not *that!*" Tennley shouted. "We have to plan our lives! You need a job! I need a better job than what I have now! Did you maybe ever consider that we should plan on moving in together?"

Andon tried to breathe. "If you felt like this," he said, "you should have just come over so we could talk about it."

"I wanted to know if you would think about our future without me making you think," Tennley retorted harshly.

"I *have* been thinking about our future."

"Ha!" Tennley sounded on the verge of getting hysterical. "Really, now? What *have* you been planning?"

Andon knew this was it. This was the last chance he would have to set things right. He forced all the tension and frustration that had been building within him away with a single breath. For the first time in the last few days, he was able to step up to Tennley and look her confidently. All of his silly panic episodes and nervous mess-ups were gone. Standing in front of her, just the two of them instead of some rehearsed idea, felt right.

"I know I've messed up," he started. "I know you're angry, and you have a right to be. I'm sorry. But I love you, Tennley. Despite what you might think, I have been taking everything into very serious thought."

With that said, Andon sank onto one knee and, finally, opened the ring box and stared Tennley straight in the eye.

"Will you marry me?"

Tennley looked baffled, completely taken aback. So many emotions flashed through her eyes; surprise, love, confusion, sadness. She hid the emotions by turning her back to him and hiding her face in her hands. Andon didn't move an inch. His heart and thoughts raced, but he waited for Tennley to recollect herself. He watched her run her hands through her hair, appearing stressed. It took a minute for her to recompose. When she did, she turned around with red-rimmed eyes.

"Andon—" Tennley's voice broke and she cleared her throat. "Andon, I'm sorry. Do you think that proposing will fix things? That getting married will change everything? Are you doing it just because I'm pregnant? If so, you don't have to do that. It won't make anything better. You just got out of *jail*, Andon. You can't just . . . You can't . . ."

"No." Andon could see tears coming to her eyes, and he desperately got to his feet. "You don't understand. I—"

"I understand perfectly, Andon," Tennley interrupted. "But this isn't right. If we're going to get married, it has to be for the right reasons, not because it might solve our problems. You're too unstable right now, Andon. I'm going to have a baby. I need someone who I know will be secure. I'm sorry. I . . . I have to go."

Leaving her purse and scattered items on the other side of the room, Tennley wiped her eyes and darted out of the apartment. Andon couldn't find it in himself to run after her. He knew he'd regret it, but he just couldn't. He'd tried and failed to win Tennley so many times; he didn't think he could handle failing again. Feeling as though he were in a deadened state, he collapsed on the couch.

Andon didn't know how long he stared at the sapphire ring. It had been the first thing he'd seen when he'd awoken in his living room the next morning. He hadn't made a single move other than to shift the ring around in his hands and watch intently as the light reflected off it.

It was almost noon when the phone rang. Andon reached to unplug it, but paused when he saw the ID. It was Keiren. Keiren was immature and could be far beyond the line of frustrating, but he was also the closest person Andon had and probably the only one he could talk to right now. Andon picked up the phone and received the call.

"Hello?" he said.

"Hey!" said Keiren. "You sound tired. Did you just wake up? Anyway, I have good news! I found the owners of that apartment you broke into—it was easy, what with all the gossip—and told them everything that happened. They thought it was hilarious and agreed to drop charges! All we have to do is pay for the window . . . You're quiet. Are you okay?"

"Tennley and I broke up."

Now it was Keiren who fell silent. Andon rubbed his temples. Just saying the words out loud made the situation feel more realistic, something he hadn't wanted.

"Wow," said Keiren. "I . . . I don't know what to say. When? Why?"

"Last night," said Andon. "She was waiting here after you drove me back. I don't know why. Something about my card, the baby, our future, and something about me being insecure."

"Emotionally or financially?"

"Not a clue."

"Wow," Keiren said again. "That's really tough, Andon. Do you want me to come over? I can bring fattening foods and some drinks."

"Thanks," said Andon, "but not today."

"Okay," said Keiren. "Understandable. Too soon. What are you going to do? You're going to try to get her back, right?"

"I don't know," Andon admitted. "She made the situation sound permanent. Maybe I should just give up. Once Tennley sets her mind, that's usually it."

"You can't do that!" said Keiren. "Not after all you went through for her! You're just upset, you don't mean that. Besides, what if she changes her mind but is too stubborn to admit it? You have to be the one to persuade her."

"I don't know, Keiren." Andon ran his hand through his hair, gripping it roughly and closing his eyes.

"Well, just think about it," Keiren said firmly. "It's not like you can return the ring or anything. You have time."

"I never asked how much the ring was," Andon realized. "How much do I owe you?"

"He sold it cheap," said Keiren. "One thousand dollars. Said he never wanted to look at it again. Don't worry about it, though. I didn't have that much cash on me, so I gave him your banking information. It's already paid off. I knew you wouldn't mind. It's worth well over ten thousand."

Andon agreed. For such a beautiful, well-crafted ring, that was very cheap. He found it surprising that it had fit his budget. Then, suddenly, something clicked out of place.

"Wait," he said, sitting up. "You gave *who* my banking information?"

"The guy who sold the ring," Keiren repeated, oblivious.

"What was his name?" Andon demanded.

"I don't remember," said Keiren. "David, Bobby, William, something like that. Why?"

"You just gave some random stranger my card info?" seethed Andon.

"He wasn't a random stranger," Keiren said indignantly. "He was selling the ring. You sound angry. Did I do something wrong?"

Andon hung up. He'd let Keiren figure that question out for himself. With time and thought, he had no doubt that he would. He punched the phone number of his bank into the phone. On top of everything else, now he had to cancel his card and call his parents.

Chapter Nine

As it turned out, Keiren had caught on quicker than what Andon had anticipated. He had apologized numerous times until the tables had turned, and it was Andon feeling guilty.

"I'm sorry for losing my temper," Andon said. "I know you didn't do it intentionally."

Andon was sitting in the living room of Keiren's one-bedroom house. After they had settled their troubles, Keiren had offered to let Andon stay since he couldn't pay his rent. "Just returning the favor from high school," Keiren had insisted.

"Don't be sorry," said Keiren. "It's a thing of the past now. We've both made mistakes."

"No, I mean it," said Andon.

"So did I," Keiren said indifferently. "Hey, I have to go. I was hoping to catch someone today. Make yourself at home."

"Not a problem."

Although Keiren's cluttered house—full of various knickknacks he had collected (tools, car parts, pictures, guns, swords, bows and arrows, fur rugs, and so on)—wasn't what most people would call "homey," it gave a persona of Keiren's personality. Andon felt he fit in just fine there.

"See ya," Keiren said, raising a hand in farewell as he stepped out the garage door. The fading roar of Keiren's Mustang signified he had left.

Andon pulled the newspaper that was lying on the table closer and flipped to the "Help Wanted" ads. It was always the same frivolous openings—fast food restaurants, corner store clerks, assistant dog groomer, and things so simple that Andon didn't know people were actually hired for. It had been six years since high school, but Andon needed to seriously contemplate the option of college. The only problem was that first he needed a good-paying job to pay for college, and he couldn't *get* a good-paying job until *after* he went to college.

One by one, Andon would call the people who were offering jobs. And one by one, he crossed off the ads. Fast food restaurant: no cooking experience. Corner store clerk: apparently they could pull up his credit score. They didn't want him behind the register. Assistant dog groomer: he crossed that one off before actually making the call. Just the thought wounded his dignity.

Once all the job openings had been crossed out and the newspaper had been wadded into the trash can, Andon flopped onto Keiren's cream-colored couch and mindlessly flipped through the television. He couldn't get a grasp on anything that was on, and instead found himself wondering what Tennley was doing. It had been two—almost three—weeks since their confrontation. Was she upset? Had she gotten over their breakup? Was she moving on? Andon pulled the ring out of his pocket. He kept it with him wherever he went. It wasn't as though he wanted to cling to it; it was more a matter of he didn't want to let it go. He idly twisted it between his fingers and studied it. To think, his and Tennley's relationship had been perfectly normal until he'd bought the stupid piece of jewelry. Maybe it was the ring's fault. After all, it hadn't worked out with the previous owner, either. Andon sighed at the pettiness his thoughts dragged him through.

When Andon heard Keiren's car pull into the garage, he checked the old-fashioned wooden clock on the wall. It had been almost four hours since Keiren had left. He wasn't even surprised that much time had passed while Andon was spaced out. It seemed to be happening more frequently lately.

"Hey, Keiren," Andon called when he heard the door open and close.

"Andon."

Andon looked up in surprise. It wasn't Keiren's voice that had responded, but a very familiar voice he had been thinking about often. He stood and spun to find himself facing Tennley. She looked prettier than he remembered. Her curled hair was a softer shade of red, her freckles were more profound, and her eyes were a deeper brown. He imagined what a mess he must look with his unbrushed hair and ripped jeans.

"Tennley," he said, trying to comprehend her presence. "How did you . . . ? What are you doing here?"

Tennley's eyes shifted sheepishly to the ground. Andon noticed a faint blush brush her cheeks.

"Keiren told me everything," she said in a barely audible voice.

"Keiren . . . ?" Andon struggled to keep up with even the simplest of statements. "What did he tell you?"

"He told me about why you've been acting so crazy," Tennley answered. "Why you went to jail and . . . Well, everything about the past week or so, really. Some of it was so simple that I'd overlooked it until he brought it up. Those silly cupcakes you were making me eat, the flowers—which, I'll admit, I thought was funny . . . You didn't really break into Sarah's bathroom, did you?"

A smile slowly crossed Andon's face. "That was Keiren's idea."

"I *knew* Keiren wouldn't have asked her to marry him," Tennley said superiorly. "I can't believe I never saw the ring in the vase. That's just so . . . All of it, it's so unlikely . . . You didn't seriously try to propose to me during a hockey game, did you?"

Andon recognized the slight smile and teasing tone in Tennley's expression. Without consciously meaning to, he grinned. After the immediate shock of seeing her after the fight, talking to her felt natural.

"Guilty," he said, giving a small shrug of his shoulders.

Tennley laughed, making him smile wider. It felt like it had been months since he'd last heard it. He was amazed at how easy it was to transition into a comfortable conversation.

"And the wine I turned down in the restaurant?" Tennley asked. "The ring was in it?"

"Yes," said Andon. "You have excellent timing on when to administer news."

Tennley giggled. "And you actually bought the ring the night of my family's dinner?"

"That's true as well."

"And you crashed through my neighbor's window, trying to reenact some stunt?"

"Unfortunately, yes."

"I can't believe you, Andon," Tennley stated, looking at him with amused weariness.

"Don't forget the last time."

"What was that?" Tennley asked, looking genuinely perplexed.

"I asked you at my apartment," Andon reminded her.

Tennley's smile faded into a grim look. "We need to talk about that."

She walked around the back of the couch and sat. Andon remained standing, feeling more comfortable facing her.

"After Keiren's story," she began, "I started getting a new look on everything we talked about. I was thinking about it on the one-hour drive here, actually, and concluded that I *might* have been a little unfair by not talking to you first."

"Might?" Andon persisted.

Tennley gave him a look that plainly told him not to push it. Andon obliged and sealed his mouth.

"Anyway," Tennley continued, "now that a baby is involved, any decision we make is going to create a big impact on our lives. I want to know if you're aware of that."

"Of course, I am," Andon replied. "I'm not *that* ignorant."

"I know," said Tennley. "I'm sorry. But how much would you be willing to change to keep up a family?"

"I'd change everything," Andon said honestly. "There's nothing I wouldn't be willing to give up other than Keiren, but I'm sure even you don't mean to go as far as to defriend him . . . Uh, right?"

Tennley bit her lip. "Well . . . Don't you think he's a little too irresponsible to be around a baby?"

"Tennley!" Andon exclaimed, surprised by her words. "He's like family!"

"Okay, okay," Tennley said quickly. "We'll talk about it later. What about moving?"

"Moving?" Andon repeated for clarification. "As in moving in together?"

"Yeah," Tennley said slowly, nervously. "And maybe out of the city, too."

"But why would we move while our lives are here?" asked Andon. He'd frankly never grasped that concept.

"It's not safe for kids," said Tennley. "I don't want my kids locked up inside all day, getting addicted to video games because I'm too afraid to let them ride their bikes on the street."

"I rode my bike on the street all the time," Andon said convincingly.

"Andon," Tennley sighed.

"All right," said Andon, "we can talk about that later, too."

"And our jobs?" Tennley continued.

"I'm working on that."

"What about the possibility of marriage?"

"I've *been* working on that."

Tennley's lips twitched upward ever so slightly.

"I'm serious, Andon," she said. "I don't want to go through what Tori and Brian did."

"Didn't they just get married?" Andon asked, cocking an eyebrow.

"Almost," said Tennley. "Tori caught Brian kissing a bridesmaid an hour before the ceremony. They broke up."

"Oh," said Andon. "That's very unfortunate."

"Exactly," said Tennley. "They just rushed right into marriage without a clue of what they were doing or what they wanted. I don't want to do that. I want plans, a foundation."

"We don't have to plan every detail right now," Andon said comfortingly. "We have time. We can plan as we go and make it work for us."

"But what if it *doesn't* work?" Tennley persisted.

"It will," Andon said confidently. "I promise."

Tennley sighed and looked down. Andon noticed a frown tug at her lips. Whether she was frowning at the situation or the spaghetti stain on the carpet, he was unsure. He remained silent, letting her make the next move in the conversation. When she looked up again, she had a slight smile on her face, but she didn't say a word. Tennley made a slight head inclination, which he responded to by tipping his head to the side. He understood when she smiled a little more and nodded to his right hand, which he now remembered was still holding the ring. He shuffled his sneakers and twirled the ring around his fingers. With a silly lopsided smile, he knelt in front of Tennley for the second time.

"Tennley," he said, smiling more at how cheesy he sounded, "will you marry me?"

He finally placed the elegant ring into Tennley's palm. She didn't shriek in surprise, understandably, but her expression was contemplating, as though she were still considering accepting the ring in front of her. Andon waited for her answer, only to have it returned to his own hands.

Andon froze in place. His lips were slightly parted, as though his mind had something to say but his mouth wouldn't oblige. His proposal had just been rejected. After all that . . .

After the longest and most painful seconds of Andon's life, Tennley finally said, "It's tradition for you to put the ring on my finger yourself."

Andon stared at her blankly. She laughed and extended her fingers. A wave of relief spread through Andon's numb body, once again allowing him the ability to properly function.

"Tennley," he repeated yet again, sliding the dark-gemmed ring onto her contrasting pale finger, "will you marry me?"

"Yes."

CPSIA information can be obtained
at www.ICGtesting.com
Printed in the USA
BVHW082032200819
556354BV00001B/43/P